From

The Wc
124 Shoreditch

Suniti Namjoshi

Born in India in 1941, Suniti Namjoshi has worked as an officer in the Indian Administrative Service, as a research assistant and in various teaching and lecturing posts in India and Canada. She has taught in the Department of English at the University of Toronto since 1972.

She has published numerous poems, fables, articles and reviews in literary and Women's Studies journals in India, Canada, the U.S. and Britain. She has published five books of poetry in India and two in Canada, *The Authentic Lie*, 1982 and *From the Bedside Book of Nightmares*, 1984, both published by Fiddlehead Poetry Books, University of New Brunswick. Her first book of fiction, *Feminist Fables*, was published by Sheba Feminist Publishers in 1981.

SUNITI NAMJOSHI

The Conversations of Cow

Illustrated by
Sarah Baylis

The Women's Press

First published by The Women's Press Limited 1985
A member of the Namara Group
124 Shoreditch High Street, London E1 6JE

Copyright © Suniti Namjoshi 1985

Illustrations copyright © Sarah Baylis 1985

British Library Cataloguing in Publication Data

Namjoshi, Suniti
    The conversations of cow.
    I. Title
    823   PR9499.3.N25
    ISBN 0–7043–2870–4
    ISBN 0–7043–3979–X Pbk

Typeset by MC Typeset, Chatham, Kent
Printed and bound in Great Britain
by Nene Litho and Woolnough Bookbinding
both of Wellingborough, Northants

For Christine

Contents

I
The Manifestation

I'm down on my knees, waiting for the goddess to manifest herself. When I open my eyes, The Cow of a Thousand Wishes is standing before me on green turf. Daffodils and crocuses grow at her feet, though, incongruously enough, the cow herself is a Brahmini cow. I like her for that. But what exactly am I to do with this goddess? Make a friend of her? A travelling companion? I look dubiously at her bony back. I pat her shoulder. I rub her forehead, the area between her curving horns. At last the cow betrays that she is alive. She blows on my shirt. I take a step or two back.

'O Cow,' I say, 'would you care to be my travelling companion?'

'What are the terms?' inquires the cow.

'Negotiable,' I answer. 'Perhaps as we stroll we might discuss the matter?'

Cow and I walk the length of the park. We would like some information about our future partners, but where to begin?

'When did you come to Canada?' I ask.

'Oh, a few years ago. How did you know I was an immigrant cow?'

How not to be personal? Or rather, how to be personal and politic as well?

'I'm from India myself.' I wonder if this constitutes a *non sequitur*.

'Oh,' says the cow. It evidently does.

'Well, it's your horns,' I continue. 'That astounding curve. It is not typical of Western cows.'

'Yes,' she answers. She sounds complacent.

I feel at a loss. 'Well, what shall we do?'

'Let's go to your place and talk.'

'Sure,' I say, but I'm thinking about the furniture. It was constructed primarily for humans.

'There are steps,' I venture.

'That's okay,' she answers. 'I can handle steps.'

I note that she uses certain Americanisms. We amble along.

*

A week later. Cow drops in for a drink again: scotch and water, very colonial — but in a finger bowl.

I am trying to find out how she survives.

'What do you live on?' I blurt it out.

'Welfare,' she replies. 'Not as good as the pickings in

14

cow drops in for a drink again

India. There one is supposed to be worshipped as a god, not that one is – but the climate is warmer.'

'Do you get a cheque? How do you sign it?'

'I am not illiterate.' That obviously is that.

She proposes to me that I go with her to visit some friends.

'They're cows,' she says. It's a statement of fact, but I suspect her of finding my ignorance culpable. I resolve to make a good impression.

'Borrow a van. They live in the country.'

She might have said 'please', but I rent a van and we drive east till we come to a field of Hereford cows. The Brahmini cow leaps a fence and skips up to them. I feel an absurd surge of national pride. She looks so graceful compared to them. I wait to be called. There is much nuzzling and nodding among the cows.

At last she returns. 'Have you any credentials?'

'Driver's licence? Credit cards?'

'No, stupid. SPCA, Greenpeace, membership of the zoo, that sort of thing.'

I haven't. We're stuck.

'You might tell them I'm wholly vegetarian?' I make the suggestion diffidently. Cow gives me a sharp look.

'All right,' she says, turning abruptly. We start walking towards the others.

'I ought to tell you,' Cow informs me, 'that this is a Self-Sustaining Community of Lesbian Cows.' I scrutinise

Cow. So, Cow and I have something in common.

The largest cow says 'Hello' to us. 'I ought to tell you
. . .' she begins.

'Yes, I know,' I say. Have to watch these interrup-
tions. But let's get on with it. 'How do you manage
about children?'

'Aı.' Well, there's brevity.

'What about property rights?'

'We're fighting it in the law courts.'

'How,' I begin — how not to be rude? — 'How did you
acquire the land in the first place?'

'Willed. Once upon a time there was a strong-minded
lesbian who was determined to leave her all to A Good
Cause.' This is Cow number two. It's time for introduc-
tions.

'I'm Suniti,' I say.

'Su? What?'

I tell them again. They get it wrong.

'Well, we'll just call you Sue for short, just as we do
Baddy here.' Her real name is Bhadravati. I look at Cow,
who looks away. Later she says to me, 'Well, you have to
adjust.'

But right then and there I say distinctly, 'No, you will
not call me Sue for short.'

There's an awkward pause. They tell me their own
names.

'I'm Boudicca,' says the largest cow. Perhaps she

detects the beginnings of a smile. 'I liked the name,' she says simply. I'm quite disarmed.

'I'm Cowslip,' says the second cow. 'I do most of the negotiating for this community of ours. I have to pass.' I look at her. She looks like a very cow-like cow.

'Hi,' I say. 'Very pleased to meet you, Cowslip.'

'Very pleased to meet you too, Snooty.' My jaw muscles tense. I'm a little surly with the other three cows. Their names it transpires are Lou-Ann, Ariadne and Sybilla – Sybbie for short.

'So, you're both from India,' says Lou-Ann. 'That's really great.'

'Why is it great?'

'Why, well, it just is, you know. You must tell us all about it.'

'It's very nice,' I say with deliberate inanity, which I think I intend to be slightly insulting, but they don't notice.

'Oh, I've always wanted to go to India. I dream about it. Only last night I had a really beautiful dream.' Sybilla, of course.

She tells us about it – at some length. The only thing that is at all clear is that she herself plays a prominent part.

Boudicca decides it's time to be gracious. 'Why don't you have supper with us and stay overnight?'

My heart sinks, but Baddy is looking hugely delighted.

Baddy and Sunny — where will it end?

'Sure,' she says. 'Thanks.' I conjure up visions of boiled dandelion soup. No, not even boiled. The fact is I am not a vegetarian. But then, this is not the time to make confessions.

Supper is as bad as could possibly be expected. I can eat almost nothing. I watch Baddy hoping she won't notice and guess the reason, but she's engaged by Ariadne. They seem to be flirting. I am becoming increasingly bad-tempered. It occurs to me to ask for some milk. But as I glance up at the cows, I'm suddenly overcome by an odd shyness. I say nothing at all, and try to swallow some oats and cold water.

At last Lou-Ann notices. 'I have a package of rusks, you know. I picked them up in a store downtown. Perhaps you would like them?'

I accept gratefully. Boudicca and Lou-Ann express concern, 'You ought to make sure you get plenty of greens . . .'

We talk about food. I am very careful; I think it would be better to discuss something else. I make the attempt, but Sybilla interrupts.

'I had a dream the other day,' she tells us calmly, 'in which I had turned into a Carnivorous Cow.' Everyone is listening. 'The odd thing is,' she goes on, 'I really enjoyed myself.'

'I had a curious dream too,' I put in nervously. 'About

a Glyptodon . . . an extinct mammal . . . an early ancestor . . .'

'What did you eat?' Baddy asks. No one is listening to me, even I am not listening. We are all waiting for Sybbie's answer.

'A birthday cake.' Poor pathetic Sybbie. I feel relieved, but Baddy is relentless.

'What was it shaped like?'

'Well,' Sybilla looks vague, then she points at me. 'It was shaped like her, except, of course, it was pink and white.'

My hands and feet have grown icy cold, but the best offence is defence I decide. No, the other way about.

'And did you carve her up?' My tone is inquiring.

'No,' says Sybbie. She sounds perfectly innocent. I can't tell whether she means to be malicious or is merely stupid.

But Lou-Ann has decided it's best to get it over with.

'And then what happened?'

'Well, we all sang happy birthday and I nibbled her toes.'

'And then?'

'Then I woke up.'

Ariadne seems strangely excited. 'But what did her toes taste like, Sybbie?' She really wants to know.

Sybilla considers. It's obvious she is trying to remember the taste.

'They tasted salty,' she says thoughtfully, 'like peanuts.' Oh, Sybilla.

The others are now willing to let the matter drop, and Baddy has moved over to sit beside me, but I no longer want her sympathetic looks. I am very cool. I speak to the cows in my most detached (but authoritative) manner: 'As you know, cows are generally regarded as a herbivorous species. Any change in their habits would certainly be disastrous.'

Baddy has a nasty look in her eye. 'Yes,' she answers, 'it would change the world balance.'

Boudicca takes charge. 'It's time to clear up,' she says, getting to her feet, 'and to find a bunk for our guests.' There's a slight emphasis on the last word. Baddy and I try to make ourselves useful. I think I've behaved badly, but it doesn't seem fair. I feel cross.

Apparently Baddy and I are supposed to sleep next to each other. I move as far away from her as I can, but later in the night it gets cold. I curl up closer. She puts a hoof lightly on my shoulder.

*

'Baddy,' I say casually, the next morning, 'I'm very hungry. I'll just run into town and get some breakfast.'

'My name is Bhadravati,' she answers formally.

'I'm sorry,' I reply. 'I'll just run into town . . .'

'I'll go with you.'

How to explain that I do not want Bhadravati to go with me? 'Okay,' I acquiesce. 'Come on.'

We drive to a pizza place, we walk in, and sit down, B as best as she can.

'I would like a vegetarian pizza, please. Anything for you?' I ask B politely.

'Yes,' she says, 'I like pizzas.'

'Two pizzas, please.' What I really wanted was a juicy hamburger . . .

The pizzas arrive, and so does the manager.

'Everything all right, sir?'

'Yes, thank you, but I am not a "Sir", I am a lesbian, and my friend is a cow.'

'GET THAT COW OUT OF HERE!'

I draw myself up to my full height. (He's still a foot taller.) 'That cow is a citizen of planet earth. If you throw us out, I shall complain about you to the Human Rights Commission.'

But he's thrusting his chest right into my face. Cow gets up. I slink past. He stands in the doorway yelling at us. I feel beaten.

Inside the van I discover that B has appropriated the pizzas. We eat them silently and return to the farm. We tell the cows what happened to us.

'Oh,' says Cowslip. 'You said who you were. You must learn how to pass. Let me explain.'

We're in for a lecture. Cow and I settle back.

'The world, as you know, is neatly divided into Class A humans and Class B humans. The rest don't count. How they look, walk and talk depends on television, but there are some factors which remain constant for several years. For example, Class A people don't wear lipstick, Class B people do. Class A people spread themselves out. Class B people apologise for so much as occupying space. Class A people stand like blocks. Class B people look unbalanced. Class A people never smile. Class B people smile placatingly twice in a minute and seldom require any provocation. Now, it's quite obvious that cows have all the characteristics of Class A people. Our very size and shape take care of that. Your best bet is to let them assume you are one.'

'Is that what you do?' I ask Cowslip.

'Yes,' she says, clipping the word, and stands there with her four feet firmly planted.

I essay a smile, but Cowslip's face remains expressionless. It's a demonstration. I am, in fact, quite impressed, but not convinced. If I understand her correctly, she seems to be suggesting . . . I would like to question her, but do not dare.

Later that morning as we're driving back, Bhadravati is very quiet. 'What are you thinking about?'

'Oh nothing,' but finally she tells me. 'I'm wondering whether cows are really like men.' The thought doesn't please her.

'Perhaps they have more in common with women?'
This suggestion seems to please even less.

*   *   *

B spends the night at my place. At about six in the
morning I hear her knocking about in the kitchen
downstairs. 'Looking for oats,' I think sleepily. There's a
tremendous crash. I discover B in a pile of cans. Now I
remember the corned beef. B is furious.

'You're an unscrupulous liar,' she tells me briefly.
Then she walks out.

I dress quickly, gulp some tea, and set out after B. I
walk up and down the streets. I ask people, 'Have you
seen a large white cow anywhere?' Most of them pretend
not to have heard me. A small brown woman in desperate
search of a large white cow — well, I suppose, to put it in
their terms, it is weird. I walk into a restaurant. The only
other occupant is a large white man chomping away at
the edge of a pizza. I stare at him. The set of his shoulders
is somehow familiar . . .

'Baddy!' I shout. I clap him on the back. Baddy glares
at me. 'Baddy, I swear I'll never touch beef again. I was

25

corrupted in North America. You know quite well
Hindus don't eat beef . . .'

The waiter comes up. 'Give the lady a hamburger,'
Baddy growls.

'Yes, sir.'

The hamburger arrives. I leave it untouched. Baddy
finishes the entire pizza. I give her my wallet, Baddy
pays, and I follow her out. Outside the restaurant she
winks at me, then she remembers she's angry with me.
She frowns.

'Baddy,' I plead with her. 'We've got to talk.'

In reply she grunts. She sets off down the street with
an appalling swagger, jostles everyone; one or two people
are knocked off the pavement. I follow in her wake. At
the street lights Baddy crosses on a flashing green. A
sports car comes to a screeching halt. The driver is a
woman. She yells something. Baddy yells back, 'You
fucking cunt!'

I'm horrified. I'm no longer sure I want to talk to
Baddy, but we're at my house.

'Baddy,' I say to her, 'You're not a man, you're a
lesbian cow. How could you say that?'

'Who are you calling a fucking cow? Ha!' she says and
again, 'Ha!' Then she grins. 'Did you see her face?' she
asks mischievously.

I am not amused. I did see her face, that is why I'm not
amused. I repeat my question, 'Why did you say that?'

the set of his shoulders
     is somehow familiar...

'It was part of the role.' She has started to drop her American accent; she looks uncomfortable.

'But there are all sorts of men, Baddy. If you had to pass, why couldn't you have passed for a gentle one?'

'Haven't got the money.'

'Baddy! That's no answer.'

'Yes, it is.' Suddenly her American accent is back. 'Okay,' she says, tossing her horns carelessly, 'next time I'll be a real gent.'

'Your manner, Baddy, is less than penitent.'

'So's yours, Sue. So's yours,' she answers rudely. 'What about that mess in the kitchen there?'

This reminds me that I'm still hungry. I put all the cans of beef into the garbage. Then I open a can of asparagus.

*

For the next two days Baddy and I are not on speaking terms, but on Wednesday morning I discover a number of packages waiting for me on my writing desk. Cow stands by. She grins at me and points at them.

'These are for me?'

Cow nods.

'How did you get them?' I think there's something about my tone she doesn't much like. The American accent is back again.

'Waal, Sue,' she drawls in exaggerated parody of I'm not quite sure whom, 'I just strolled into a drugstore and told the salesgirl —'

'Saleswoman,' I interrupt.

'Yeah,' Baddy is imperturbable. 'I told the cute little salesperson there that I wanted my girl, Sue, to make herself a bit smarter, you know, to start looking like a real woman, and so, would the cutie please help me to put together some basic make-up. No, I didn't say "please", I just told her, and she looked real pleased and started scurrying about.'

I wait till Baddy finishes. Then I pick up the parcels and impale them on her horns. Lipsticks roll about. Face powder cascades over Baddy's face and a trickle of eye-liner runs down one ear. She looks extremely funny. I begin to laugh. At the same time I notice that she is crying.

I apologise. 'Look, Bhadravati, I'm sorry,' I say. 'It was just your manner. It put me off.'

I fetch damp paper towels and wipe her face. We sit down and drink some tea. She's still snuffling, but I'd like an explanation.

'It was very sweet of you to get me these presents,' I say patiently, 'but — by the way, how did you pay for them?'

'Your credit cards,' she mutters obscurely into the paper towels. I let that pass.

'Yes, well, as I was saying, it was very sweet, but what's the point? What were you doing?'

'I was trying to make you into a Class B human.' She says it just like that. The answer, of course, is obvious. But to hear it said shocks me somehow.

'But why, Bhadravati? Don't you like me as I am?'

'Yes, of course I do, Suniti.' Bhadravati is entirely serious. 'But you see, we have to survive. And I thought that perhaps if you dressed up as a Class B human and I dressed up as Class A, we'd manage better. We could have adventures, see all sorts of things. Won't you consider it? We'd learn a lot.'

I do consider it. I sulk for an hour, then I sneak up to the bathroom and try on the make-up. After a while I even begin to enjoy myself. At last I'm satisfied. I descend the staircase and show myself to Bhadravati.

'How do I look?'

'You look charming,' she says.

I preen a little.

'But your skin is still brown.'

'Yes?' I say, challenging her, but Bhadravati is in a good mood.

'It's all right.' She winks at me. 'You'll pass.'

'Bhadravati, let's try it out. Let's go for a walk.' I'm very excited.

B rises. She opens the door elaborately for me. We set out. An elderly gent tips his hat to us, his elderly wife beams at us. Everyone seems to approve of us. I feel so good, so safe, so respectable . . . I belong!

Later that night my conscience bothers me. 'B,' I say, 'what about our identities? Aren't we being false to our true selves?'

'Oh yeah?' she mumbles absent-mindedly, her eyes are glued to the television set.

'B!' I insist.

'What? Oh.' She turns down the volume. 'It's all right,' she says, 'identity is fluid. Haven't you heard of transmigration? And you call yourself a good Brahmin?'

I don't, as a matter of fact, but I let that pass.

'But, B, aren't you really a lesbian cow?'

'Well, I don't know,' she says. 'That seems rather exotic . . . What's wrong with being a white man?' But she sees I'm upset. She stops teasing me. 'All I ever wanted,' she says seriously, 'was to be an ordinary animal.'

'Oh but you are. You're perfectly ordinary —' I stop short. Then like an idiot I try again. 'When I first saw you, B, standing four square in that green field, I thought you were a goddess.'

'And so I am,' she says complacently. I'm stunned. But her mood changes.

'Go on,' she says, poking me in the ribs. 'Go on. You're putting me on.'

I realise it's hopeless to try to carry on the conversation. B will become more and more facetious, Baddy will emerge, who knows where it will end.

'Good night,' I say. I go to sleep, and I dream. Bhadravati and I have undergone plastic surgery. We have the faces of women and the hindquarters and legs of Brahmini cows and we wear top hats like true gentlemen. We're walking through a forest looking for something. At last we sit down and villagers approach us and put garlands of flowers about our necks. They want our blessings. I feel embarrassed, but Bhadravati is most gracious. She blesses them lavishly and also gives them our top hats. Then our wings slide out and we drift heavenwards. As we're drifting I can feel the sun warming my back. I have the strongest possible sense of good-will towards everyone and every blessed thing.

I decide not to repeat my dream to B, then do so anyhow.

'Well, now we know who you really are,' she chortles happily, 'Saint Suniti without her top hat.'

I make a face at her, but don't say anything.

*　　*　　*

Three days later B confronts me.

'Suniti,' she says, 'you're essentially a dreamer, but dreams and conversation are not enough. Let's do something.'

'What?'

'Have you any money?'

'Sure,' I say. 'I work for a living, you know.'

B is curious. 'What do you do?'

'I teach English Literature.'

B laughs.

'Just because I'm a woman and a foreigner, it does not follow I cannot be a university professor.'

'And a lesbian,' B adds, looking mischievous. 'But really,' she goes on, 'English Literature?'

'Onlookers,' I tell her loftily, 'often see more than participants.'

But B isn't listening. 'If you have money,' she says, 'we could do something. Money is power. Money transforms.'

'I haven't very much,' I interject hastily. 'What do you mean, money transforms?'

B shrugs. 'Super Cow today has an independent income.' It's obvious she has been watching TV again, but for the moment she offers no elucidation. Still, if I know B, she'll return to the subject. A couple of hours later, she does.

'Suniti,' she says, 'will you give me some money?'

Her directness is startling. I hedge. 'What do you want it for and how much?'

'I want to go on a journey. I want 500 dollars.'

I am not sure that B understands money at all. 'How far can you go on 500 dollars?'

'Oh, at 50 cents a mile, about one thousand miles. One can do a lot with 500 dollars.'

'What?'

'One can hire ten able-bodied women to work ten hours a day for ten days at 5 cents an hour.'

'That's 5,000 dollars, B. But what good is that?'

'You buy their time and add it to your own. This means that you've extended your life by one thousand hours.'

'Oh, B, what nonsense. What else?'

'Oh for heaven's sake, Suniti. Can't you understand that money is power? You can fly through the air. You can treat a supermarket like a giant treasure trove. You can have three wishes and a bit left over. You can, if you like, become invisible. You can buy life and time and energy. You can make people do what you want.'

'Within limits.'

'Yes, of course. Money is quantifiable. It depends largely on how much you've got.' B is getting impatient with me.

'But, B, if money is power, why should I give it to you?'

'Because you like me.'

I try again. 'But, B, if money can do all that, isn't it better to use the money to buy more?'

'More what?'

'More money.'

'Miser!'

I explain to B that I sell my time, in other words, my life, to make money. I want to save some so that eventually I'll have an independent income. B nods.

'What will you do with your time then?'

'Write.'

'Dreamer!'

'What's wrong with dreams?'

'They make nothing happen.'

B goes away. I shake my head. B is behaving like a penniless adolescent. I daydream. What if all adolescents were princely heirs? I think of my cousins in India. I think of my friends in Canada, of their shopping sprees, of the joyful and sudden expenditure of power. Do they feel like giants? I feel muddled. Wouldn't it be nice to go up to B, give her 500 dollars, and say, 'Here, B, here's a little power. Go out and spend it. Use it up.' It would make me feel magnificent, it would give me such a jolt of power. I feel terrible.

But B isn't done with me. She returns to the room and sits there looking insufferably patient.

'What's the matter?'

'This life you're leading, has it occurred to you that it's too sheltered?'

I'm instantly wary, but I temporise. 'Well, perhaps you're right. Let's do something.'

'What?'

'Let's think of a project.'

'What sort of project?'

'A dream. A realistic dream. World Peace. Non-discrimination Against Lesbians. Vegetarianism. That sort of thing.'

B is annoyed. 'Do you think that's funny?'

'No, I apologise. It was — it was almost a kind of despair. What is needed is a transformation.'

B relents. 'The trouble with you is you're not practical.' (She's wrong. I'm very practical . . .)

'Well, what about something more specific,' I venture, 'for instance, the single-minded pursuit of personal happiness?'

'Please be serious.' B is getting angry again.

'I'm sorry, B. I am trying to be serious, but I'm frightened. I think that is what's making me facetious.'

'What are you frightened of?'

'Of the tangible. The tangible dream is a real threat.'

'Oh don't be silly. You're frightened of everything and when you can't find anything . . .' She trails off and walks up and down in exasperation. 'Don't you ever enjoy yourself?' I've decided to sulk and don't answer, but B continues, 'You really must learn to face your fear. What is it that you're so frightened of?'

Doesn't she know? I'm terrified of people.

'B,' I say suddenly, 'let's throw a party. Let's have fun.'

B is mollified, but I'm in for it now. I look at her. She's smiling. She doesn't seem to realise how awkward it's going to be. What am I to say? 'Friends this is Cow, Cow this is Friends'?

But when the time comes that is exactly what I do say.

＊

It's a small party. I've invited three of my colleagues. They are mostly white – I am not colour conscious – and entirely liberal, of this last I am sure.

Peter arrives first. He's always punctual. Sometimes he drives round the block or waits in his car till the exact hour. A real gent – an example to Baddy. I wonder how he and she will get on.

I introduce them. B, I notice, has decided to be gracious. She smiles at him. They talk solemnly about the joys of the country, the pleasures of pastoral. B occupies the entire sofa. She has thrown a turquoise and gold Benarasi stole across her shoulders. She looks magnificent. Peter, as usual, is being shyly gallant. I think about dinner, and the fact that the food will be vegetarian. I earnestly hope no one comments.

But when Julia arrives, the first thing she wants to know is what's for dinner and will the dessert she has brought prove suitable. We admire the dessert, and Julia congratulates me on my newly found vegetarianism. B doesn't look at me. She and Julia discuss salad, while Peter looks benignly on.

Well, I needn't have worried. Cow evidently has considerable charm. They don't seem to have noticed that she is a cow. Perhaps they all have excellent manners? I, myself, feel rather excluded. I go into the kitchen and toss salad. We drink more wine. Julia says she is getting hungry, so does Cow. Peter, as usual, looks patient. I explain apologetically that we are waiting for Kate. The telephone rings. A domestic disaster. Kate is going to be very late. We should start dinner.

They all eat hungrily and say how much they're enjoying the food. I don't say anything at all. I toy with the salad. Half-way through Kate rushes in. She gives us a vivid account of her freezer overflowing. The food-supply people brought too much food. Cabbages and cutlets cascaded down the pavement. 'Oh,' I think, 'Oh, Cow isn't going to let that pass, not without comment.' I flee into the kitchen. But when I return they're deep in a discussion about cryology. Cow is saying that she doesn't envy the frozen mammoth. It's a kind of immortality she herself would not want. I just stare at them.

Then I hear Kate speculate, 'I wonder if the flesh of the

mammoth was still fresh?'

Now surely there will be a row. Don't they realise that
Cow is an animal? My palms are clammy. I feel a little
sick. By the time I recover, Cow and Kate are happily
discussing mutual consent: whether it's all right to eat
meat if there's mutual consent between eater and eaten.
The others are listening with smiles of amusement.

I give up. I decide to stop worrying, until over coffee I
hear Cow expounding an obscure version of the Theory of
Reincarnation. One becomes what one has eaten. For
example, if one has eaten a great deal of beef, or a great
many snails . . . They are charmed by the concept. As
Peter says, 'It offers one a measure of self-determination.'
And Julia adds, 'And constant control, the sense that
destiny is in one's own hands.' Kate is looking mildly
wistful – undoubtedly concocting an exotic diet.

At last they leave, I wave feebly. Cow has been a great
success. My nerves are in shreds.

*　　*　　*

The following day Cow is still in an excellent temper.
'That was a pleasant dinner party.' She beams at me.

'Let's have some more. Haven't you got any other friends?'

'Er. Yes. Sure.' I pretend my mouth is full of porridge. Luckily, she drops the subject. But she's in an expansive mood, and I take advantage.

'B,' I say casually, 'were you ever in love?'

'Good heavens, yes!' A reminiscent smile crosses her face. She leans back to talk, but it wasn't her reminiscences I was leading up to.

I interpose a question. 'Did all your affairs end happily, B?'

She's startled. 'Well, no,' she admits, 'in that they ended, it was an unhappy end if you see what I mean — in that an ending is an unhappy thing.' I like to see her stumble occasionally. She looks less smug. We brood for a moment.

'B,' I say suddenly, 'I think I'm becoming a misogynist.'

'What?'

'You know, a misogynist — a hater of women.'

'I see,' she replies. 'Well, that's rather awkward since you are yourself —'

'A woman. Yes, I know. Sometimes I think there's been a mistake. The wrong soul in the wrong body. That sort of thing.'

'Well, who do you think you are then?'

'Perhaps a cow.'

'A male cow or a female cow? A lesbian cow or a heterosexual one? Pedigreed or non-pedigreed? Which particular one?'

I look at B to see if she's mocking me, but she's merely looking politely interested.

'Well, perhaps not a cow,' I say hastily. 'Perhaps I'm a snail.'

'A snail?'

'Yes, they're bisexual.'

'And as a snail, do you like other snails?'

'I like eating them.' It's an honest answer and has slipped out of me before I could stop it. To my horror my mouth is watering, and I can taste garlic butter.

But Cow's gaze remains dispassionate. For a while we don't say anything. At last she asks, 'Why do you hate women?'

'Because they hurt.' That slipped out too, I didn't mean to say it.

'What? All of them?'

'No, only if one happens to fall in love.' I can no longer look at B. I stare at my hands, but when she speaks, her voice is gentle.

'Suniti, what's wrong? What exactly is the matter?'

'Oh nothing much. Sometimes I think it's impossible to get on. Got involved with someone. Didn't work out. Broke up. You know, the usual sort of thing.' I mumble this rapidly.

B's voice still sounds gentle. 'Suniti,' she says, 'what do you want?'

'A drug, a dream, a facile perfection.' By this time I am so embarrassed I take myself off to bed and eventually fall asleep in a terrible temper.

In the morning I apologise to Cow for my childish behaviour, but she doesn't seem angry, merely points to a bottle standing on the table. It seems to be filled with vitamin pills. They're bright yellow.

'What's that?'

'An aphrodisiac.' I can't tell if she's joking or not.

'How does it work?'

'You take one a day. Then you and the world fall in love with each other.'

'What? Just like that?' I'm slightly shocked by the lack of discrimination, though I do not say so.

'No, it isn't that good. It doesn't always work. But it is quite good. Do you want to try some?'

'Have you ever tried it?'

'Oh sure. I eat it by the handful.'

I suspect now that Cow is teasing me. I eye the bottle and try to articulate a disquieting thought. 'Cow,' I say at last, 'how does one know when it has worked, whether, in fact, it has worked or whether it hasn't?'

'Ah,' she says smilingly. 'That's the beauty of it. One doesn't.'

I try to smile back, but I feel angry. Cow has been

mocking me. I stalk out of the house. When I return that evening, Cow tries to talk to me.

'Why are you angry with me?'

'I'm not. Just tired.' I am not going to expose myself to such silliness further.

'Oh come on, Suniti. Don't be absurd. Do be sensible and tell me why you're angry.'

'Life is absurd. As for being sensible, the thing to do is to drop the matter.' I make my voice sound quiet and dignified. I straighten my shoulders.

Cow is smiling. 'Don't be so cross. Come and sit down and talk to me.' She sounds coaxing.

I say wearily, 'There really isn't anything to talk about. We're both tired. Let's go to sleep. Good night.' I make my exit feeling very patient, very long-suffering and very serious.

*

That night I dream. Cow has transformed herself into a woman. She is wearing a sari and sitting on the lawn of a large house under a banyan. She is feeding chipmunks. A crow squawks somewhere. I can hear sparrows. A couple of mynahs are feeding on the lawn. I sit there gazing at Bhadravati. I feel such admiration and love for her. She smiles at me. I approach closer. The chipmunks run away, but she strokes my forehead, she ruffles my fur. I

44

I am an excellent animal...

feel very clean and alive and healthy. I'm a well-kept poodle. I sit at her feet and look at her quietly. I'm an excellent animal. When she rises to go into the house, I walk beside her up to the door; but since she hasn't called me, I stay outside and chase chipmunks.

II
Bhadravati

When I wake up the next morning, I resolve not to say a word about the dream. I feel vulnerable.

She's sitting at the breakfast table wearing a sari. The April sun is shining on her hair. She's very beautiful. I recoil a little, though my body keeps walking. I enter the room. I don't want to deal with this. Why did B have to change into a woman?

'You've changed?' I say non-committally, but with a slight inflexion.

'Yes,' she says. 'Do you like it?'

'It?'

'The change.'

'Oh yes, well, of course.' I'm dithering. 'But, of course, B, you are always you whoever you are — if you see what I mean.' What on earth do I mean?

But B is smiling. 'Well, come and sit down. Would you like some tea?'

'Yes, please,' I answer. I must pull myself together. B is obviously in charge. I can't let her have it all her own way. I must say something, be something. What's the right tone? What's my best bet? I decide to be formal.

'Thank you,' I say when she brings me my tea. At all costs one must be polite. 'Did you sleep well last night?'

'I dreamed,' she says, smiling at me full in the face. Her beauty gives her so much assurance. I hope that none of this shows on my face.

I manage to ask with mild interest, 'And what did you dream?'

'I dreamt I was in India again. I was playing with the chipmunks. I had a dear little poodle . . .'

I'm frightened. Is she mocking me? But she isn't even looking at me. She's staring into space, seeing herself in the sunlit garden.

I decide to be brave. 'What was the poodle's name?' I even look at her.

'Her name?' B says. 'Let me think now. Su—, Suzanne! That's right. Her name was Suzy. She was so loving, so intelligent.' B smiles as she thinks about Suzy.

My mind is made up. Whoever I become, I'm not going to be a poodle. If necessary, I shall be churlish. But what stance should I take? What should I say next? I wish B wasn't quite so beautiful. It's hard not to look at her. She might notice. I feel resentful. What happened to Cow? And where's my friend Baddy? I feel uncomfortable. If only I could work up enough resentment. If only she wasn't so very attractive. Perhaps I should be Baddy?

I decide to be myself: simple, sincere, earnest Suniti.

'B,' I say looking at her frankly. 'Why have you decided to become a woman?'

'Because I felt like it.' Her tone is all wrong.

I try again. 'But, B, don't you see how awkward it is?'

'Why is it awkward? It's usually much easier to explain away a woman than to explain a cow.' Her voice is so reasonable, her smile so friendly.

'B,' I say in sudden exasperation, 'if you're going to be a woman, I'm going to be something else.'

'What would you like to be?' She seems genuinely interested.

'A goldfish!'

I can see her considering the matter. She's imagining the bowl, the exact shape, size and colour of the fish. She looks dubious.

'A goldfish? Are you really sure you'd like to be a goldfish? It seems so confining.'

I push back my chair and stand up. 'I have to get to work,' I say shortly.

All day long I think of B. What exactly am I supposed to do? And why is there a problem? What difference does it make that she is no longer a cow? What's the matter with me? I feel resolute and angry. I decide to do nothing. I shall treat B exactly as though she were B, which she is, who she was, well as she would have been . . .

When I get home that evening, I slap her on the back, 'Come on, B. Let's eat out and go to a movie.'

B looks startled. 'Suniti,' she says, 'since when have you adopted this hearty manner?' She isn't angry, just puzzled.

I look sheepish, then catch myself at it. First a poodle, then a sheep. Where will it end? 'Sorry, B,' I say lightly, 'I was just being friendly.'

'I've made dinner,' she informs me. 'Let's eat and then I want to talk to you.'

'About what?'

'About being a goldfish.'

Dinner is excellent, though it is vegetarian. I find myself thinking, 'Though she's no longer a cow, she's still vegetarian, and still Indian, is she still . . .?' I break off the thought and eat. B helps me to more rice. 'I feel like a guest in my own house,' I think bitterly. I hope my face is looking civilised.

'Dinner was excellent,' I say politely. 'Thank you.'

'Good,' she replies. 'Now let's talk.'

I brace myself, then say I need a drink. 'Would you like one?'

'No thank you.' Oh Baddy, Baddy, gone are the days when you downed your whisky and talked fake American.

'You used to like scotch.'

'I still do.' She seems amused.

I sit down. 'Well, what did you want to talk about?'

'About you, Suniti. You haven't really been yourself today. I'm worried about you. You're behaving so oddly.'

'But I'm very much myself,' I say in feigned surprise. 'See, same person, same body.' That last remark is intentionally pointed. B ignores it.

'But you seem distant somehow. Are you hiding something?'

'Oh, you know me. 'Tis my secret sorrow. I'm an incurable romantic.' I'm not quite sure who that was supposed to be. I'm losing control. I had better do something.

But B puts a hand on my arm — oh wicked B. She sounds sincere. 'Suniti,' she says, 'what's the matter with you? Why are you pulling away from me?'

'Oh it's all right,' I growl. I get up, and slouch about. 'Just have a headache, feel a bit bearish.' So now I'm a bear? She fetches aspirins.

'Sit down. We really have to talk, you know.' I sit obediently.

'Now,' she says, 'why did you say you wanted to be a goldfish?'

'Oh I don't know. It's an experience. One must not be afraid of experiencing a new thing. You were saying only the other day that my life was too limited, too boring.'

'But a goldfish, Sue?' Why is she calling me Sue? Suddenly I'm angry.

'Why are you calling me "Sue"?' I demand.

'I'm sorry, Suniti. It just slipped out. Don't be so sensitive.'

'Perhaps I should be a pachyderm?' I mean to be sarcastic.

But B only answers, 'Well, yes, that's a possibility. What else have you thought of?'

'A bear, a sheep and a poodle!' I shouldn't have said that. It's time to take this conversation by the horns so to speak and steer it around.

'B,' I say to her, 'why did you decide to stop being a cow?'

But B is looking at me with a dawning realisation. 'So that's what's bothering you. I see.' Her voice trails away. 'I see . . .'

I wish I was something small and fluffy. I wish I could hide in B's sari, bury my face in B's shoulder. I wish B would cradle me. I feel like crying. And then to my horror, I am crying. That's not it at all. That's not what I meant to do. That's not what I meant to be. B cuddles me.

After a while I wash my face and blow my nose. 'I feel like a fool,' I tell B.

'Never mind, love,' she says comfortably. 'These transformations are always hard. You'll get used to it.'

I go to bed, I dream that night that Cow has returned to tuck me in. And as she sits there, I hear her murmuring, 'I had forgotten you were a misogynist.'

*

But it's B who wakes me. 'Come on,' she calls out. 'Wake up. We're going.' I dive under the bedclothes. I know I look scruffy early in the morning.

'Going where?' I mutter from under the bedclothes.

'On a holiday.'

I get up and dress. I come to the conclusion that I might be better off as a thick-skinned herbivore. I say so to B. She doesn't seem surprised.

'Oh all right. We'll see about that when we get where we're going.'

'But where are we going?'

'To see a friend. She's wise and kind and lives in the country.'

'What about my work?'

'The term is over. As for your writing, you can do it there.'

'Who else will I meet?'

'You'll meet my sister.'

'Your sister!' How to ask B whether her sister is a cow or a woman? 'B, what's her name?'

'Her name is Charlotte.'

'How can that be? How can her name possibly be Charlotte, particularly if she's a Hindu?'

'Well, she's English. Now do get ready.'

'But, B,' I persist. After all, I like to know exactly what I'm doing. 'What's going to happen? Are we going on a quest?'

'A what?'

'You know, a journey of exploration. We undergo ordeals, and then I find out who I really am.'

'Is that what you want?'

'Yes.'

'Well, as far as I'm concerned, we're merely stepping into the next province to visit friends.' She smiles. 'Still, it's just possible you'll get what you want . . .'

I feel nervous. I dare not ask any more questions.

*   *   *

At first I'm glad that I'm driving; I cannot look at B, I have to look at the road ahead. We stop for coffee. While the car's being filled, the garage mechanic chats with B — oh, about nothing much — about the weather. I feel resentful. Why do I have to do the driving? And to pay for everything? Coffee and petrol, for instance. Inside the café I complain bitterly that my neck hurts. B is sympathetic.

'Shall I drive?'

'Sure, if you would like to.'

B takes over. She's a far better driver than I am. I try not to look at her. I stare out of the window. When we get to Montréal, we check in at a hotel, and B pays. I hope she hasn't been reading my thoughts. I try to make polite conversation. Where does she get the money anyhow? We walk about the city and have dinner. The following morning, as I understand it, we're to drive further. Her friends are expecting us. But there are a number of things I'd like to know; I can't quite find the right words.

We spend the evening at a lesbian bar. B makes friends with half a dozen women. I sit down and feel like a lump. I understand only a tenth of the French. But B is being kind to me; she introduces me to the other women. They decide for some reason that my name is Sulky. What a nice name. I'm patted on the back— nice Sulky — then ignored. After a while I say I'm sleepy and we return to the hotel.

'This can't go on,' I tell myself. 'You should never have agreed to this trip in the first place. But now that you have, do pull yourself together and try to be pleasant.' I breathe regularly, count to 500, and fall asleep.

Oddly enough, the following morning I feel cheerful. The sun is shining, B is still B, I am still me, the people we're going to meet might prove interesting; and besides, since one must be something, one might as well be cheerful.

B has changed into slacks and a shirt, and looks more ordinary. What am I saying? But she does. I am less in awe of her. And the driving and the countryside and four cups of coffee have put me in a good humour.

When we arrive at the farmhouse, Charlotte is standing outside the door ready to greet us. She is tall — at least six feet two inches — and very fat. Her blue eyes laugh, her blonde hair blazes in the bright sun. She and B embrace one another like long-lost sisters. I can't understand how they can be sisters, but they seem to be. I stand there awkwardly waiting to be introduced; but when we are introduced, Charlotte gives me such a friendly smile that I smile back at once. We troop into the house.

Margaret is also tall, but slender, like an egret perhaps, or a heron. She smiles at us shyly. I feel we have interrupted her, but she makes us welcome. This involves kissing us on both cheeks, which I rather like, but since I'm not sure I want to admit to this, I look solemn.

Suddenly I hear music, just a bar or two, bird-like and clear. It enters the room, stays for a minute, then exits abruptly. I look at Margaret.

'Oh that,' says Margaret. 'That's Madeleine. She's very elusive. You'll meet her at dinner.'

Meanwhile B has disappeared. Margaret indicates the open window. B has changed into Cow again. She and Charlotte are walking in the garden. Charlotte has her arm about B's neck. They look peaceful. I don't quite know what to do with myself. I am occupying space. Margaret sets me to chopping vegetables.

Charlotte dashes in and grabs a sandwich. She calls out something over her shoulder. Margaret explains, 'She and Bhadravati haven't seen each other for a very long time. They're lunching together.'

Margaret and I sit down at the table. Margaret smiles. 'Madeleine probably won't be joining us. She's bird-like in her habits. And at the moment, of course, more so than ever.'

I would like to ask why, but it might be rude.

But Margaret understands. 'You see, she's in love.'

I don't really know how to respond, so I smile. There's a long pause. At last I ask, 'With whom is she in love?'

'Ah,' says Margaret. 'That's uncertain. Sometimes I think she's in love with the weather. But the important thing is that she is in love.'

I find myself telling Margaret about Baddy's love philtre. Margaret listens attentively. I like Margaret. She makes me feel sensitive and intelligent.

*　　*　　*

At dinner that evening B has changed into a sarong and kurta. She looks fresh and clean, like a wood nymph. It's easy to imagine her in the wooded valley below the house, provided, of course, that it was always summer. She also looks more mischievous, less responsible. But Margaret's face is as kind as ever, as is Charlotte's. The empty place is for Madeleine, who still hasn't appeared. We begin without her.

B says in a conversational voice, 'Suniti is a misogyn-ist.'

I could kill her for that. And I had so wanted to make a good impression.

But Margaret has turned her slow blue gaze inquiring-ly at me.

'Do you hate all women all the time?' she asks.

How to answer? I look around the table. Charlotte nods encouragingly. 'It must be hard work,' she murmurs.

'Well, no,' I mumble. But they're waiting for me to go on. 'Only some, some of the time.'

I feel miserable, but they're not going to let the matter drop.

'And how do you feel about men?' Charlotte asks.

'And birds?' Margaret inquires.

62

they look peaceful...

'And wood nymphs and goddesses?' B continues.

'Well, I don't like men very much. Birds are okay, I guess. And I don't know much about nymphs and goddesses. Wouldn't know one if I saw one.' I reply sullenly. I might as well give up. They're never going to like me now. I feel I'm being got at, and I want to say, 'I don't care. I don't care if they don't like me because I don't like women.' I feel stupid and absurd.

'At which times do you dislike which women?' Charlotte again.

'When they make me feel stupid. When they hurt.' I know I'm making a fool of myself, but don't seem to be able to help it.

'There, there.' Margaret pats my shoulder.

'Suniti is very sensitive,' B murmurs.

When I've stopped snuffling into my napkin, and they think I'm sufficiently recovered, they turn on me again.

'Suniti thinks she would like to be a cow,' B says as though in explanation.

They take up the thought with a flattering enthusiasm that I could do without.

'She thinks that cows are thick-skinned,' B adds.

They study me intently. I know they are asking themselves whether or not I would make a good cow. I can feel myself fading under that threefold glance. I make an effort.

'It doesn't really matter whether or not I would make a

good cow,' I tell them firmly. 'The point is, do I want to be a cow?'

'Well, do you?' they ask simultaneously. At this moment they seem to me like three witches. Heaven knows what's going to happen. I'm saved by Madeleine. The door blows open. She dances in rather than walks in. When she takes her place, she smiles enchantingly. I forget everything. I am dazzled. I would stare unblinkingly, but the light seems to flicker whenever she moves. I stare none the less as best I can.

B kicks me under the table. 'Suniti,' she says. 'Do wake up. You look exactly like a little owl.' I wake up and smile vaguely.

Madeleine laughs. 'It's the light,' she says. 'When one comes in out of the dark, the light dazzles.' I don't explain that I haven't been in the dark, and for once the others let it pass.

'Where's X?' Margaret asks.

For a moment Madeleine's golden eyes lose their light. 'Oh X,' she says blankly. 'X is gone.' Then her eyes light up. 'But she'll be back tomorrow.' I try to imagine X.

'I would like,' I say suddenly, 'to be a mysterious stranger.'

'Oh, Suniti,' Margaret is kind. 'You are very exotic.'

'But I don't want to be exotic, only mysterious.'

'How mysterious?' Charlotte wants to know.

'Very, exceedingly, excessively mysterious.' I feel

light-hearted. Anything can happen. Anything is possible. But when I look again, Madeleine has left. I feel despondent.

'Who is X?' I ask casually.

No one answers. B and Charlotte seem to be waiting for Margaret to speak. At last she does.

'No one quite knows, but it's generally believed that she is Madeleine's lover.'

'But who *is* X?' B kicks me, and I realise I'm persisting to the point of rudeness, but I don't care. I ask again, '*Who* is X? What does she look like?'

Charlotte says, 'No one really knows, but it is generally thought she is supremely beautiful.'

'Oh,' I say. For the moment I have no more questions.

When we've finished dessert, Margaret clears her throat quietly. 'It's time,' she says.

They are all looking at me. I look blank. B kicks me under the table. I turn on her. 'B, that's the third time this evening you've kicked me. Please don't do it.'

But B merely says, 'We're waiting, Suniti.'

'Waiting for what?'

'Your transformation.'

'My what? But what's it about?'

'Your quest for being. That's what you've always wanted, isn't it? To Be Someone?'

I'm taken aback. I didn't know that that was expected. I thought we were merely on a pleasant weekend.

'Well, what am I supposed to do?' I feel helpless.

'Make an intelligent wish, a really well thought out one.' Margaret answers. Unlike B, whom I suspect of mocking me, Margaret looks serene and gentle, but she also seems to be entirely serious.

'Can I do it tomorrow?' I suggest feebly.

They appear surprised, but since they don't say 'No', I take it to mean that I have till tomorrow. What have I got into? What was B's intention?

*

B and I are sharing a room. She takes the large bed and I take the small cot near the window. It gets chilly. I feel cold. I complain. Also I'm worried and can't sleep. At last B takes pity on me and lets me into her bed. It's warm and comfortable, but I don't quite know whether or not I can put my arms round her. She gives no indication. I still can't sleep. I get out of bed and walk about.

One of these days I'll deal with B, but right now I need to know what's going to happen.

'B,' I say, 'I can't sleep.'

'Well, you had better try or you'll be tired tomorrow.'

'But, B, this wish I'm supposed to make, what's it about?'

'Oh, you know, who you are and who you'd like to be.

What it is you really want. The sort of thing you're always moaning about.' B is mumbling into the pillow.

'But, B, I'm thoroughly muddled about who I am; and as for what I want, I really don't know.'

In answer B merely grunts.

'B,' I plead, 'please help me.'

'Oh all right, Suniti.' B sits up. 'Now, what do you want?'

'That's just it, B. I'm not sure I know.'

'Well, you said you wanted to be a cow.'

'I'm not really sure. Cows are so cow-like. Then I needn't be me. I thought it might be restful.'

'You would like to be someone else, it that it?'

'Well, yes, or different.'

'How?'

'Well, bigger, better, stronger.'

'Be all that. What's stopping you? Be bigger, better, stronger, etc.'

'But it's hard work.'

'Then that's not what you want?'

I decide to change the subject a little. 'B, if I make this wish, will I get what I want?'

'You can say what you want, we'll try to corroborate you.'

'You mean like indulging a lunatic? So that if I suddenly say, "I am Napoleon," all of you say, "Yes, dear, and so you are!" '

'No, it's more like a play. So that if you have costumes and the props, and the setting is right, for a while you have a functioning system.'

'Well, but what if I'm Napoleon, and you're Baddy, and Charlotte is an Englishwoman, and Margaret is a Brahmin, and Madeleine is an ambience, then what? Then what happens?'

'Oh for pity's sake, Suniti. You have an arbitrary order. Do go to sleep.'

'B?'

'Yes!'

'I don't want to be Napoleon.'

*　　*　　*

The following morning Margaret takes me for a short walk. I trot along, sometimes before her and sometimes behind her. I feel like a small dog. It's perfectly possible that I am one. I am glad that Margaret doesn't make conversation. That would require me to say something, to choose an attitude, a tone, an inflexion. I toy with the idea of being a talking dog, the life of the party, a prize poodle. I decide in favour of being a strong silent one. But then I see some water. I would like to be a duck. I feel very duck-like. I try to tuck my head into my shoulder — to see what it feels like — and catch Margaret watching me. 'I feel very duck-like,' I inform her. Margaret smiles her acquiescence.

After lunch I lie down on the grass. I'm quite convinced that the grass doesn't mind being crushed, that it doesn't object to the weight of my body. I decide that Margaret, Charlotte and Bhadravati are daisies and Madeleine is the yellow sun. X is a shadow. Or perhaps she's the night? Or perhaps they are both aspects of the moon? I don't much mind, but just as I've almost fallen asleep, I hear voices. Charlotte and B are sitting near by. I listen. I wonder if they're going to talk about me? Then I scold myself for being such an egoist. They do talk about me.

'Where on earth did you find her?' 'Her' — they must mean me.

'In a park in Toronto. She was kneeling on the grass. She looked so peculiar that I walked up to her. When she opened her eyes, we got into conversation.' Well, I suppose they do mean me.

B giggles. 'She thought I was a goddess.'

'And so you are.' This from Charlotte.

'Yes, but not in the sense she thinks I'm one.'

'What do you propose to do with her?'

'Oh, I don't know. She's not a bad sort really.'

'She's prickly and difficult.'

71

'Oh, she's all right when her ego's unruffled.'

'Yes, but that's all she is — a transparent ego and some sensations and impressions.'

'Exactly.'

'What do you mean?'

'She has potential.'

'For being someone?'

'No —'

But at this point I can't take it any more. I sit up and glare at them.

'I am *not* merely a transparent ego.'

'No, that's true enough,' Charlotte smiles pleasantly. 'On occasion, I'm sure you can be quite colourful, indeed, "a woman of colour".'

'That's racist!' I exclaim.

'I'm sorry,' says Charlotte penitently. 'I couldn't resist the play on words.'

I feel annoyed. 'But I must be someone,' I point out to them. 'You can't very well have had a conversation about no one, can you?'

'No, dear,' B's voice is deliberately soothing. It makes me furious.

'But aren't we all an accidental conglomeration of arbitrary particulars, duly supplied with a functioning ego?'

'Suniti, what a good description!' I stare at Charlotte. I'm astonished to find that she really means it. I feel mollified. I smirk, then remember to frown, but I feel better.

We go in to tea. Charlotte and B are attentive. They ply me with chocolate cake, which I don't particularly want. Still, it's a nice gesture. After several cups of tea, Elizabeth asks gently, 'Have you thought at all about who you'd like to be?'

I look at her cunningly. 'Could we have a practice run?'

I don't think that that's what either of them really wants to do, but I think they think they owe it to me.

'Certainly,' they say. 'Go ahead.'

'Well then,' I tell them, 'I would like to be a Lover.' I had hoped to startle them with sheer effrontery, but they seem unsurprised.

'Whose lover would you like to be?' Charlotte, politely.

'I'm not quite sure. I would like a choice.'

'Like a proud potentate with a largish harem?'

'No-o.'

'Well, how then?'

I look them in the eye. 'From whoever's available.' They begin to understand and I think they'll be angry, but I find they're laughing, B particularly.

She says, 'You mean you want us to lie about while you strut up and down and make your choice?'

'Well, no, not exactly. B, you're not angry, are you?'

'What for?'

'Well, for suggesting . . .'

'That one of us might be your lover? Was it intended as an offensive suggestion?'

'No.' I stare hard at the floor. 'But these things can be offensive.'

'Why?'

'Cultural context. It's a way, you know, of humiliating women.'

'And this bothers you? Do you, as a misogynist, wish to humiliate your fellow-women?'

'No. I am one. I don't wish to humiliate anyone . . .' I mutter confusedly.

'Well, what do you want?'

'A lover,' I mumble.

'Do you mean you want a lover or you want to be one?'

'She means both,' B says briskly. 'Come on, Charlotte, let's get on with it.'

They drape themselves on the living-room sofa. B points to a large cushion. 'That's Margaret over there. She's busy at the moment. And if you want Madeleine, she'll have to be imagined. That is her nature.'

I just stand there and stare at them.

Charlotte gets impatient. 'Well, come on, Suniti, do get on with it. Behave like a lover.'

'What? In public? In front of everyone?'

'Well, at least it will give you a sense of audience.

74

How can you know that you've done something unless the thing is seen to be done?'

I don't quite understand this, but I force myself to walk over to B.

'You're very beautiful,' I say inanely.

'Yes. Well.'

'B,' I snap at her. 'You're not co-operating. What on earth am I supposed to say if you just say, "Yes, well"?'

'All right. What should I say?'

'Well, I suppose you should say something reciprocal.'

'So are you.'

'So am I what?'

'Beautiful.'

'Ah.' I can't think of anything to say. I throw up my hands. 'B, it seems hopeless. I don't feel like a lover, I feel like a fool.'

'Well,' B answers, 'it may be, you know, that that is the kind of lover you are.'

'Oh.' I feel utterly dashed. I sit down. Charlotte walks over and puts her arm about me.

'Oh, Suniti,' she says, 'you look so very like a damsel in distress. I will be your lover. I will carry you off and lock you in a castle and protect you from everything for ever and ever.'

I'm startled. 'But I don't want to be abducted and imprisoned for life. Who would?'

'Sorry,' says Charlotte, 'I was only being gallant.'

I turn on them indignantly. 'Where do you get your notions anyhow?'

They look surprised. 'We get them from you. Having this practice run was your idea.'

'Well, where do I get them from?'

'I suspect,' says Charlotte, 'that you get them from being a student of literature.'

They both seem amused. I am close to tears. I go for a long walk all by myself. But when I come back in time for dinner, at least I'm prepared and a little in control.

Towards the end of dinner Margaret asks the inevitable question, kindly enough, but there's no evading it. 'Well, Suniti, have you decided who or what you want to become?'

'Yes,' I answer smiling happily. 'You'll find out tomorrow.' Then I grin at them. 'I already am. Tomorrow I become.' I feel so cheerful, I dance like Madeleine, I flutter like a bird. 'I can be anything, anyone,' I collapse on the floor in a small huddle, I peer at them coyly, 'or no one.'

Margaret, Charlotte and Madeleine clap. I make a mental note that even no one can be a good performer. Bhadravati helps me up, and we go for a walk. She disappears among the trees. I follow her.

III
Interlude

The air seems tangible. I can smell it and breathe it. And it has colour, it's the solid night permeated by the moon. I can hear Bhadravati ahead of me. Sometimes a leaf rustles, a twig cracks.

'B,' I call out, 'B, don't walk so fast. You're losing me.' She calls back something, but I can't understand it. I stumble after her.

I don't know whether or not I am happy. I don't know whether I'm supposed to follow her. I sit down under a tree, I rub my cheek against the bark. It's an evergreen of some sort, not a tamarind or a peepal, but the bark is pleasant and rough. I think I am happy. I listen to the night sounds. There's a light breeze. A cricket near by is making a terrific racket. I think I can hear B's voice. I lie down on the ground. Stars overhead. When I look through the trees again, I can see her watching me. She is beautiful. She is like the trees.

She comes and sits down close beside me. 'Suniti,' she says, 'what is the cricket saying?'

I tell her, 'The cricket is shouting. The cricket is saying how beautiful you are, how beautiful it is. It is saying, "I want to come close and lie down beside you." It is saying, "Pick me up, Suniti. Pick me up in the palm of your hand and stroke and caress me and I'll sing for you." '

'What nonsense. Crickets aren't eloquent.'

'Oh yes, they are. They say anything and everything. You know that. Do you know, I like this tree I'm sitting under.'

'It's a pine,' she says factually.

'A pine, a cricket, a moon, a forest, two women . . . Who am I, B?'

'Sometimes I think you're a baby.'

'All right, I'm a baby. I'm an intelligent baby with a transparent mind. Tell me a story intended for babies.'

She shifts slightly so that my head now rests in her lap. I'm not altogether sure whether it's B or the night that holds me so close.

'Once upon a time,' she says quietly, 'there was a Spindly Cow. Her taut white hide was stretched across a bony frame. She was large and reasonably good-looking, but she was hollow inside. There was a blackness inside her, an incessant craving. She decided that it would be her mission in life to assuage that darkness, to become substantial. So she ate everything she saw, pots and pans, kettles and crayfish, cabbages and turnips, articles of clothing, houses and furniture – you know, just ordinary things one sees all the time.'

'B, did she eat animals?'

'Yes, animals too – men and women, pigs and parrots, tiny little babies, tigers and terrapins, everything. Luckily, she was a careless animal and short-sighted too, so that she left a great many things only half-eaten, and then there were a great many more that she didn't even see. Still, she was persistent and she crunched steadily. The earth began to lose its shape and looked more and more like a pock-marked lump. At last the creatures who were left decided it was time to say something. "O Cow," they said, approaching her as closely as each of them dared.'

'Did they all speak together?'

'Yes, you mustn't interrupt, particularly not when it gets exciting.'

'Sorry.'

' "O Cow," they said, all of them at once, "you have now consumed a fifth of the planet. Is the hunger within you at all assuaged? Are you satisfied?"

' "No," said Spindleshanks, because that was her name. "No," she said with her mouth full, because that was her nature. "It's become a habit. But I'll tell you what I'll do. I won't eat you as long as you give me something else to eat."

'So the creatures went away and ploughed the earth,

and built factories, and in times of scarcity cast lots among themselves in order to decide who should be sacrificed. But the business of casting lots didn't work well, and there were arguments among the creatures, and disputes and discussions, and a few minor scuffles, then a great deal of fighting and finally huge wars, through all of which Spindleshanks chomped her way steadily.

'At last there was only a handful of creatures left and only a small patch of earth for the cow to stand on.'

'Oh, well, then she must have realised what she'd been doing and stopped doing it – when she saw the blackness of space underfoot, so to speak.'

'No, she didn't. And, Suniti, you really mustn't interrupt.'

'But, B, surely the few remaining creatures must have been driven to do something?'

'No, they weren't. The Cow ate them up, the very last handful and the last clod of earth.'

'And then?'

'And then there was nothing. Only Spindleshanks. Spindleshanks and Nothing. Nothing and Spindleshanks. She felt terrible. She began to scream. She screamed and screamed until she burst and had turned herself inside out. Then the world spilled out of her, all higgledy-piggledy, and not quite the same world as it once had been because it had been processed by Spindleshanks and Spindleshanks permeated everything.'

clothing, pigs and parrots, tiny little babies...

and turnips, articles of

pots and pans, kettles and crayfish, cabbages

SHE ATE EVERYTHING ...

'And the blackness?'

'The blackness was now both outside and inside. And Spindleshanks herself, fragments of Spindleshanks were a part of the world.'

'And then what happened?'

'Why, the world carried on, but a different world.'

'Thank you for telling me the story, B.' But B is quiet. 'Has it a moral?' I ask slyly.

'No, no moral.' Her voice sounds sad.

I don't say anything. I caress her lightly, so lightly that I think perhaps she will think it's the breeze. When I sense that her sadness has lifted a little, I ask her gently, 'B, if you cut me open, what would you find?'

She smiles. 'Crickets and cockroaches, the carcasses of dead animals, pine trees and peepal trees, giraffes and ostriches, forests and rivers, entire bestiaries.'

'Do you mind, B?'

'No, I don't mind. I'm glad of it.'

'But you've forgotten something.'

'What?'

'The watch-dog, a poodle or a puppy, or even a cow, but functioning always as a guardian or a lackey, a self-appointed porter, and always with the same question, "Is this thing good or bad for me?" '

B laughs. 'And getting it wrong most of the time. If you were to cut me open, Suniti, what would you find?'

'Blood and guts, a functioning body, a living

creature.'

'Will it do, Suniti?'

'You know it will.'

That night B and I become lovers. The birds wake us up the next morning. They're hunting for food. They are very noisy. They are celebrating the fact . . . well, they are celebrating the world.

IV
Bud

For the next two weeks I live in a daze. My soul, such as it is, seems to be extended over the entire countryside. My ego, vigilant as ever, but careless now of its old duties, is concentrated entirely on Bhadravati. She's in the air I breathe, the taste of water. I know that this cannot go on for ever, but time seems to have turned into a golden haze. The sun and moon are our friendly companions, as are Madeleine, Charlotte and Margaret, who is a kindly host and offers the comforts and convenience of her house.

But on the fifteenth day I find myself asking, 'B, what are we going to do next? What are we going to become?'

'Become?'

'Yes, oughtn't there to be a logical pattern? One significant event following another? Now that we are lovers, ought we not to get married for example?'

'But, Suniti, two women can't get married. You're being carried away by literature.'

'No, by life actually. Ought we not to settle down and

have children?'

'Ought?'

'Well, it's usually done.'

'Do be sensible.'

'I am being.'

'No, you're being conventional.'

'What's wrong with that?'

'It's – it's arbitrary, my dear. Well, who would we be?'

'Well, we could be Mr and Mrs Someone. Mr and Mrs Suniti, for instance.'

'What?'

'Why not? Canadians can't tell the difference.'

'So you'd like to be Mr Someone. Suniti, what do you know about being a man?'

'In theory quite a lot. That's what literature is all about – the nature of man. In practice very little. I've come to the conclusion that men are aliens.'

'But you'd like to be one?'

'No, I didn't say that. I was just looking for a possible pattern.'

'Oh, Suniti.'

'Well, what do you think, B?'

'I think we ought to explore the matter, the Men from Mars, the Unearthly Aliens.'

But I don't pursue the conversation. It has begun to trouble me. The golden haze seems to have dimmed. I'm aware that we've stayed with Margaret for over a fortnight. We came for a weekend. We cannot go on living here for ever.

*

At dinner that night Margaret and Charlotte look as usual. Madeleine has disappeared. B looks different, still recognisable, but — dare I say it? — less beautiful.

She says casually, 'Suniti thinks that men come from Mars.'

Charlotte is interested. 'Ah, do you think that they're a different species? Different from women or cows or poodles?'

I'm in for it. I say firmly. 'No, I mean that they did not originate on the planet earth.'

Margaret looks up. 'How did they get here?'

'Space-ships.' It's the obvious answer. What else could I have said?

'But what happened to the space-ships?' Margaret persists.

'Broke down. It has taken them all these centuries to build new ones.'

'In what capacity did they arrive on earth?' Charlotte wants to know.

'Invaders. This may be deduced from their subsequent behaviour.' For this bit of the theory I have adopted my driest and most academic manner.

91

Charlotte is amused, but Margaret has a question.

'But, Suniti,' she says, 'how did they adjust?'

'Not very well, surely that is obvious.' I'm feeling confident now. 'But well enough by means of mutation and biological manipulation and a massive mythologisation of the planetary purpose.'

Charlotte is staring at me. 'What first led you to the formulation of this theory?'

I grin at her. 'The study of literature.'

'Explain yourself.'

'Well, as you know, man himself is right at the centre of the literary universe. Pigs and poodles, bats and babies, women and children, the earth itself, are always "the other". Now how to explain this inexplicable division, this perverse passion to make "the other" conform to the requirements of man's desire? It doesn't make sense, unless, of course, one starts with the postulate that men, in fact, are really Martians. Then all the pieces fit together.'

There's a longish pause. Then B says, 'Suniti was saying only this morning that she'd like to be a Martian.'

'Oh, B, that wasn't quite what I said.' Damn B anyhow! Why does she always have to spoil things? Just when I thought I was impressing the others? But they're waiting for me to explain myself. 'Oh, well,' I mumble sheepishly, 'I was just saying to B that perhaps we should get married . . .' I feel like a fool. 'It, it was only a stray thought, a shadow of a suggestion . . .' I trail off incoherently. I stare at my plate.

'But that does not necessarily involve being a Martian,' Charlotte points out. Oh, what have I got into? It's obvious they're not going to drop the matter.

'Suniti wanted us to be a Mr and Mrs Someone, a Martian and His Maiden, if I have understood her correctly,' B puts in.

I must put a stop to this. 'B,' I say loudly, 'let us be clear about this. I do not, I have never wanted, I do not intend to be a Martian.'

'Oh. Why not? Well, since you refuse, I suppose I'll have to be one.'

'What?'

'A Martian. We could call ourselves Mr and Mrs Bhadravati. It has a ring to it.'

'B.' I'm doing my best to pronounce each word very clearly. 'I do not want to be married to a Martian.'

'Oh well, we can live in sin then. It's probably more modern. You can be my mistress. We could call ourselves The Man from Mars and His Reluctant Companion.'

Charlotte and Margaret seem amused. Perhaps B is joking. I hope she is joking.

'B, you must be joking? You can't be serious?'

'Why not?' she asks.

'But, B, how could you possibly turn into a Man from Mars?'

'It's really quite simple — a little padding, a little make-up and a great deal of confidence.'

My heart sinks. She may be right. I have difficulty trying to swallow my dinner.

Margaret asks gently, 'Why does the idea distress you so much?'

'Are you a misanthrope?' Charlotte asks. Her deep blue eyes are smiling so blandly, I don't know what to answer. 'In the same way as you're a misogynist?' she adds helpfully.

'Not in the same way.' I keep my answer short, but I seem to have admitted that I am a misogynist. Oh well, best to let it go.

'But these Aliens, these Men from Mars, are you not interested in them?' inquires Margaret.

'Can't help being interested,' I mumble. 'They occupy the planet, but I prefer to observe them from a safe distance.' I don't know where this is leading. I wish they'd stop.

'Are you afraid of them?' A forthright question. B, of course.

'No, I'm not exactly afraid,' I bluster.

But B won't let up. 'Then why do you keep a safe distance?'

'Because they bite,' I snap.

'Martians bite?' Margaret displays all the curiosity of an avid naturalist.

'Well, no, that's not what I mean.'

'Then?'

I have nothing to lose. I might as well say it, say anything at all.

'They rope you in.'

'Rope you in?'

'Yes, in accordance with their mission.'

'And what's that?'

'The domestication of the species of planet earth.' There, perhaps that will silence them.

'But, Suniti,' it's B's turn again, 'if the Martians are in charge, would there not be some advantage in an alliance with a Martian?'

'What?'

'Easy access to Martian circles.'

'Oh, B.'

'Besides.'

'Yes?'

'Consider how much safer you'd be if you ventured out tomorrow under the full protection of an honest-to-goodness Martian.'

I can see that her mind is fully made up, but I try pleading with her. 'Please, B?'

'It's no use, Suniti. I know what I'm doing. My mind is made up.'

I mutter to myself, 'That's what I was afraid of.' But I say nothing aloud.

When Charlotte and Margaret kiss me 'Good night', they seem particularly gentle, like mothers and sisters at a wedding or a funeral, but that last thought is probably just my imagination.

*   *   *

At breakfast B has turned into what is unquestionably a Martian. I don't like it. I scowl at first, then turn my back. B seems impervious. But when Madeleine comes in, B jumps up, hovers about her, and tries to see that she has everything she wants. The fact that B is making her comfortable in her own house doesn't escape my notice, but Madeleine refrains from pointing it out. She waits for someone to explain matters.

B suddenly sticks out a hand. 'I'm Bud, you know. Glad to meet you. And this is Suniti.' He pushes me forward.

'I believe we've met,' I say feebly. Madeleine blinks, smiles and disappears.

Bud and I are left facing one another. 'Well,' he says, 'I'll just bring down the suitcases. Then we're ready to go.'

I don't say anything, but then he hasn't waited for an answer.

While I'm waiting, Margaret and Charlotte walk into the room. I leap to my feet.

'Margaret,' I expostulate, 'you've got to stop this.'

'Stop what?'

'Bud. He has taken over.'

From the expression on their faces I can see that they understand exactly what has happened, but they don't seem alarmed.

'What has he been doing?'

'He's been drinking coffee and is fetching the suitcases.'

'Well, that's quite helpful of him, isn't it?' Charlotte offers.

'But it's the way he's been doing it.'

Just then Bud comes down. He kisses Margaret and Charlotte rapidly, says, 'Thanks for everything,' grabs me by the elbow and rushes me out, shouting, 'Come on, Suniti, let's go.'

He has the car keys and has started the engine before I can stop him.

'Just a minute,' I say. I don't want to be rude, but this is really too much. I go back to the house.

'Margaret, Charlotte, Bud has turned into a Man from Mars. What shall I do?'

'Well, you don't have to go with him,' Charlotte says.

'But he has my car keys. He's revving up the engine. What shall I do?'

'Ask him for the car keys,' Charlotte suggests.

'But that means a confrontation . . . Oh, Margaret.'

Margaret comforts me. 'It's all right, Suniti. He's still B. Why not play along and see what happens?'

'All right,' I answer, but I have my misgivings. I kiss them good bye, and look about for Madeleine, but she's nowhere in sight. I feel sadder than ever.

I go up to Bud and demand the car keys.

'Sure,' he replies. 'But you don't have to be so uptight about it, you know.'

I put the car into gear and drive off. Bud beside me wears a stolid face, he looks immovable.

After an hour or so, when we've had some coffee and I've paid for my own, I feel better, though what I object to is that his letting me pay seems a kindly concession. I remind myself that B is lurking in him somewhere, but it's difficult. He seems hopelessly alien.

When we get to Montréal and stop at a hotel, I try to check in while Bud stands quietly looking over my shoulder. But the clerk at the counter addresses him exclusively. I put it down to his allying himself with a fellow-Martian. But what am I to make of the waitress at dinner who behaves as though only Bud existed and I was furniture?

At last it's over. We can go to our room. I shall talk to Bud. Surely in the end B will emerge?

'B,' I say severely, 'this has gone on long enough.'

But Bud merely puts his arms round me and gives me a kiss.

I draw back. 'Stop it!' I exclaim.

'Why?' he asks.

'Because it's not what I want.'

'But is that important? You don't have to do anything. Just lie back . . .' As I'm about to lose my temper, his face breaks into a mischievous grin, the expression softens.

'B,' I exclaim gladly, 'B, you're back!' But when I put my arms about her, there's an incongruity — B's head and Bud's body. I sit on the bed and stare at her.

'What have you done?'

'Nothing,' B says. 'What's the matter, Suniti? You look so perplexed, and all day long you've been so very bad-tempered.'

'But your body . . .' I begin.

'Don't you like me as I am?'

'Well, yes, no.'

B is smiling. 'Do you know, the trouble with you is that you're very conventional.'

I pull myself together. 'That's not fair, B. It's not just me. When I'm with Bud in public, I become an appendage, a secondary person.'

'Oh, come on, Suniti, why not look at it differently? You share in his status. When we return to Toronto with Bud at your side, you'll be a different person.'

I hadn't thought of that.

'B,' I wail. 'How on earth am I to explain Bud?'

'There's nothing to explain. You've caught yourself a live Martian. It's perfectly normal.'

'B,' I'm pleading with her now. 'Please dispense with Bud. When Bud is around, I feel uncomfortable.'

'But, Suniti,' she says, 'that's your problem, not Bud's.'

'But he does it on purpose.'

'What?'

'Taking advantage of his superior status.'

B draws herself up. 'Bud, I'll have you know, is a nice person. And you, my friend, are an out and out snob and very status conscious.'

I feel defeated. Perhaps B is right. I feel awful. Privately I think there isn't much to choose between B and Bud.

Suddenly B turns gentle. She puts an arm around me. 'Would you like to be Bud?'

'No, I've already told you, I wouldn't.'

'There, you see, it's hard being Bud. It's generous of me to agree to be Bud.'

This is so outrageous that for a moment I can't think of an answer, but I manage to ask, 'Very well then, what are the duties and obligations of Bud?'

'Oh, the usual ones, being strong, successful, right and noble.'

'And the duties and obligations of Bud's partner?'

'Oh you mean Sue's? The complementary ones — being weak, incompetent, uncertain and inferior.'

'B, you know that's nonsense. An incompetent Sue would be useless to Bud. And in any event, I don't want to be a Sue or a Bud!'

'Yes, dear.'

'Who was that?'

'Whoever you like, dear.'

'No, tell me, who are you at this moment?'

'But if you can't tell the difference, how does it matter?'

I don't know what to say, but I have to say something. I adopt a weary and patient tone. 'Of course it matters. Bud is a Martian, B isn't.' But even I can't keep a straight face over this piece of evasion. Bud is giggling, and I join her.

I don't sleep very well. What difference does it make whether B is B or B is Bud? But it does. It makes a difference to me. B is just B, but when Bud does something, he's backed by the forces of the Martian Empire.

'B,' I mutter, prodding him in the back. 'You're backed by the forces of the Martian Empire.'

B grunts.

*

That night I dream that the Jovians have invaded. They're unthinkably gigantic and unbelievably monstrous. Buddy and I are comrades in arms and giving battle. As we cower in a cave together I feel a sudden upsurge of fellow feeling.

'Buddy,' I exclaim, throwing an arm about his shoulders, 'compared to the Jovians you don't seem at all alien.'

Buddy responds by punching me lightly. 'You're a good chap, Suniti. Sometimes I forget you're not a Martian. When the war is over, why don't you take out the proper papers? Become one of us? We'd have a good time together – two gay Martians exploring the world.'

I'm annoyed. I want to say, 'I guess I was wrong. Perhaps there isn't much difference between Martians and Jovians.' But it's the wrong time to say it. The Jovians are upon us.

*   *   *

I had half hoped that B might have tired of being Bud. She hasn't. I glare at her. But Bud is being pleasant.

'Good morning,' he says nicely. 'How are you feeling this morning?'

'Terrible thanks.'

'Why?'

'I would like Bud to go away and B to return. Oh, it's not that I dislike Bud,' I add hastily, 'but he tends to bully me. B is much nicer.'

'But that's not true, Suniti. B reduced you to a small poodle, whereas all I do is make you irritable.' He looks vulnerable and hurt. I wonder if he's about to start crying. I put an arm about his shoulder.

'Well, since you're B anyway, I'll treat you exactly as though you were B. Then I'm sure we'll get on together.'

'All right, but only in private.'

'What?'

'Well in public I have to uphold the ancient traditions of the Martian Empire.'

'Oh to hell with you!' I'm angry. At this point I don't care whether I lose B or Buddy or both.

Buddy capitulates. 'Oh, all right. I won't uphold the ancient traditions, but don't blame me if we get into trouble.'

'What do you mean?'

'Well, the Martians don't like it if any of their number goes native. There are severe repercussions . . .'

I see his point, but I'll be damned if I concede it. 'Well, it's your own fault then for being a Martian.'

Buddy looks glum. 'Yes, Suniti, it's a terrible burden.'

We breakfast in silence.

'What shall we do?' he asks at last.

'Well we can't go to a lesbian bar, not this time. You wouldn't be welcome.'

'No,' he says. 'It's not fair. Haven't you any friends who would make me welcome?' He has that little boy look again.

'Several,' I mutter, but I'm thinking in particular of Amy Rose-Blossom. She would dote on him. I telephone her.

'Come on,' I tell him. 'We'll look around the city, and later we'll pay a visit. We've been invited to lunch.'

We walk about the city. He makes a point of being conspicuously ungallant. I pretend not to notice, but I find it tiresome.

Eventually he asks, 'Who are we visiting?'

'Someone who will like you.'

'Why?'

'She likes Martians.'

'What, all Martians? Without discrimination?'

'Yes. She runs a home for them.'

'Oh you mean for the discarded and disabled.'

'She thinks all Martians are in some way disabled. Something to do with the Jovian Wars. She thinks they need to be nursed and coddled.'

'Oh. You know, Suniti, I'm not at all sure I'll get on with your friend . . .' but they get on famously. Amy makes a fuss about him, and Bud relaxes and simpers and smirks.

I leave them together after telling Bud I'll meet him at the hotel. I walk through the streets. It's the first time in days I've been by myself. I feel luxuriously anonymous.

*   *   *

But when I return to the hotel, I find that Bud is already back. He grins at me, 'Mrs Rose-Blossom's treatment does a world of good. You should try it, Suniti.'

'No,' I shake my head at him. 'The full treatment is for Martians alone. Amy says women don't need it. Amy says women are tough.'

But I feel relaxed and reasonably good-tempered. We go out to eat and are nice to each other. As we're leaving the *maître d'hôtel* says, 'Bring her again. She's beautiful.'

Bud looks smug. 'There, Suniti. Aren't you pleased?'

'No. If you went into a parking lot with a foreign car, it's exactly what the attendant might say to you.'

Bud's face falls. 'You're very hard to please, you know.'

'So are you. You'd be pleased if I were pleased. What you want is a happy acquiescence.'

'Well, why not? I could spend my life trying to please

you, and you could spend yours being pleased. We'd live happily for ever. Doesn't it sound good?'

'No, what you need is a stone companion, smiling happily for ever and ever.'

'No, what I need is a metal one, smiling happily when I push a button.' Buddy smiles suddenly. 'After all, there are times when you've wanted one too, haven't you?'

'Wanted what?'

'A robot companion.'

I consider the matter. 'Well, be one then. After all, your function in life is to please, isn't it?'

'No, it isn't.'

'But only a minute ago you were saying . . .'

'That I'd like to please you? Yes, but only when it's convenient. And not as a robot. Why don't you be one?'

'What? A robot? You'd be bored, Buddy. What would you do for conversation?'

'For intellectual stimulus I'd seek out the society of my fellow-Martians.'

'And what would I do?'

'You could join the local branch of the Robots' Club.'

By this time we're back at the hotel.

'Buddy,' I tell him quietly, 'I am not a robot.'

'Suniti,' he answers, 'I am not an alien.'

'Who are you then?'

'I think probably I'm really a woman. I would like to be one.'

I think of B, but there's no sign of her. Bud is being very much himself.

'Why?'

'It's less difficult.'

'Oh, well, what's to stop you? Be a woman then.'

'Do you think I would make a good one?'

'No.'

'Why not?'

'You have the wrong habits.'

Bud seems depressed, but he quickly recovers.

'Are you a good woman?'

What can I say? 'No,' I tell him, 'I'm an unsatisfactory one.'

Suddenly B is grinning — it is B, isn't it? — she puts an arm about me. 'Suniti,' she says, 'I'll tell you a secret, I also am an unsatisfactory Martian.'

'Oh, you do very well.' I pat her on the back.

But she feels I haven't been suitably impressed. 'I'll tell you another thing, and this is a top secret, a well-guarded one — all Martians are unsatisfactory ones.'

I laugh. 'But, B, that's a well-known fact.'

She looks put out. 'Well, at least you'll concede that you and the Martians have something in common.'

I smile, but it's an unsatisfactory solution. At last I ask, 'Are you trying to tell me that Men from Mars are really women?'

'Yes. You've got it at last.'

'But, B, why do they behave so differently from women?'

'Lack of opportunity and education, my dear.'

B is grinning, I grin back; but late that night when B asks me, 'Suniti, what would you really like?' all I can say is, 'B, I need to be by myself for a bit; I would very much like to be left alone.'

V
Conjuring Cow

When I wake up the next morning S2 is lying in bed beside me. We open our eyes in unison. We lie there wondering whether it's possible to converse with one another.

'Suniti,' we say turning simultaneously, then fall back.

'This needs practice,' we say together. 'You go first.'

I make an effort. 'I will be me, and you can be "you",' I say to S2.

S2 demurs. 'From my point of view —'

'I am me,' I finish for her. 'Yes, well, for practical purposes let's take turns.' S2 concurs.

We get up and dress ourselves with some difficulty. This constant contiguity is a nuisance. I know that S2 is worthwhile in herself, but I'm not altogether happy with this needless duplication. Still, we ought to get on. Our relationship will no doubt be entirely amicable. We smile at each other, but in spite of this both S2 and I are slightly uneasy. We decide to have breakfast in our own room and return to Toronto.

'Well, what shall we have?' I ask politely. I already know, but one might as well be courteous even with oneself.

S2 surprises me, 'Scrambled eggs on toast.'

'But S2,' I say, 'you know perfectly well I never have eggs, not for breakfast.'

'The truth is, Suniti, we seldom have breakfast, but since we decided to order some . . .'

'But I never have breakfast when I'm alone.'

'But I'm not alone. I am breakfasting with a charming woman . . .'

'Who?'

'You, of course.' I look at S2 sharply.

'You know perfectly well I'm not charming – not before breakfast.'

S2 smiles in a deprecating manner. I note she doesn't dispute the matter.

We order toast, and when it arrives we eat in silence. I have misgivings now, which are further increased at the check-out counter. She uses my credit card to pay the bill, she produces a flawless signature. I suddenly realise that for whatever she does, I am accountable. I hope she turns out to be a sensible person.

'Oh well,' I console myself, 'at least we can share the driving.'

'True enough,' S2 replies. 'I'll drive first.'

But when we stop for coffee and it's my turn to drive, I find I'm as stiff and tired as S2 herself. 'This is empathy,' I think. 'This is true fellow feeling. At last I am experiencing genuine compassion, but it's something on the whole I could do without.'

I suggest to S2 that we stop at Cow Farm — if they will have us. She agrees readily. I know she is hoping to get news of Cow. It's late when we arrive.

'Hi, we were just passing by and thought we'd look in.' I feel awkward, but Boudicca and Cowslip make us welcome.

'This is S2.' I'm afraid Cowslip is about to say 'Neat', but she doesn't, just introduces herself, and S2 I notice smiles at her.

We head towards the barn. Both S2 and I keep peering into the dark.

'What are you looking for?' Boudicca asks.

'We're looking for Cow,' S2 answers.

'Cow?' After all, there are at least five or six cows on the farm alone.

'For Buddy,' I explain.

'Do you mean Baddy?' Cowslip inquires.

'Bhadravati,' S2 answers.

'What does she look like?'

Both S2 and I pause for a moment.

'She looks like you,' S2 says.

'She looks like us,' I put in.

Boudicca and Cowslip stare at us.

'You must be tired. Come in and sit down and rest for a while. Have some oats.'

'No, no thanks. We've already eaten.' But we do go in and sit down.

I decide to try again. 'Have you seen Cow?'

'You mean Baddy, don't you?' Boudicca answers. 'Sure, she's always about. She comes and goes, you know.'

'Yes, but is she here now?'

S2 looks at me warningly. I know I'm being peremptory, but I wish these cows would be more helpful.

Boudicca and Cowslip are not offended. 'No,' they say a little sadly. 'We don't think so. She isn't here now.'

For a moment I feel ashamed of myself. For a moment Boudicca and Cowslip look almost beautiful. But all I wanted was a straightforward answer to a simple question. It's silly to waste time in inane conversation. I get up to go, but Lou-Ann, Ariadne and Sybbie walk in.

'Hi, Sue,' they greet me cheerfully.

'My name is not —' S2 interrupts me and introduces herself. I stare at her. She's positively beaming and they're smiling back.

'I've heard so much about you from Baddy,' she murmurs. To call Bhadravati 'Baddy' so effortlessly — I'm amazed by S2. I retreat into a corner and scowl.

'Oh, what have you heard?'

'I've heard about your friendliness and warmth,' she tells the cows. 'And about your dreams,' she adds turning to Sybbie.

How can she? This is crass flattery. I dissociate myself completely from her.

'I had a dream the other day,' Sybbie begins.

'What was it about?' Trust S2 to ask.

Boudicca and Cowslip have excused themselves to prepare supper. I resign myself and try not to listen.

'Oh, it was really weird.'

'Yes, Sybbie, but what was it about?' Lou-Ann prompts.

'It was about a Cow. And, you know, it was in Technicolor.'

We all wait. She realises that her explanation is insufficient.

She justifies herself. 'Well, but you see, the Technicolor was really important. Because everything was in colour except the Cow and some of the other cows, except me, of course. I was in it too.'

'What colour was the Cow?' I hear myself asking.

'Well, it depended on the angle from which you came up to her. Her left side was white and her right side was black.' Sybbie stares at me. 'You were in it too,' she says suddenly.

'And what colour was I?' I ask unpleasantly.

But Sybbie doesn't notice. 'You were no colour at all. But you were looking for a Cow.'

'And then what happened?' S2 is signalling to me to keep my mouth shut.

'Well, you asked Ariadne, "Have you come across a Snow-White Cow?" And Ariadne said, "Sure, I'll take you to her." '

'And did she?'

'Well, we took you to where the cows were. But you couldn't find her.'

'Why not?' I ask sharply.

'I don't know,' Sybbie answers. 'The Black and White Cow was right there — you looked at her for a long time — and near her there were some zebra-striped cows, and lots of grey ones mixed in among them, and dappled ones and of course ordinary brown ones like me. Oh it was a grand sight. But you started crying.'

'What!' I feel indignant. Damn Sybbie and her dreams anyway.

But S2 asks, 'And then?'

'Then Ariadne and I comforted you.'

I'm furious with myself for letting Sybbie talk. I should have known this would happen. As I'm clearing my throat to say lightly, 'What an absurd dream,' I find that S2 is giving Sybbie a hug and is saying to her, 'Oh Sybbie, you're a dear.' Both Sybbie and Ariadne look smug and even Lou-Ann is smiling complacently. I decide to keep quiet.

Finally, after a mercifully light supper, we leave. In the car, as we're driving home, S2 says, 'Well, I'm glad we stopped, aren't you?'

'Yes,' I mutter, but after a while I lose my temper.

'You're a hypocrite,' I tell her.

'And you're a boor.'

*　　*　　*

The house seems unchanged, but silent and empty. We both walk about looking for B, but there's no trace of her. We make ourselves a cup of tea and sit down.

'It's lonely without B,' I say at last.

'Yes, yes it is,' S2 sighs heavily. I wish she'd cheer up. It isn't pleasant to have a despondent companion.

'Well, you have me.'

'Yes,' but she doesn't sound at all enthusiastic.

'What's the matter? Don't you like me?'

'Oh you're all right, Suniti, but rather self-absorbed.'

'In what way?'

'Well you just sit there without saying a word, and behave exactly as though you were all alone.'

'We are all alone. I like being alone. Don't you?'

'I suppose so.'

'Well, then, what's the matter?'

'It isn't very pleasant having a despondent companion.'

I get to my feet. 'Oh, come on, S2, we're both tired. Let's go to sleep. Oh, and if at all possible, don't snore so much.'

Later that night I ask S2 timidly, 'S2?'

'Yes?'

'Do you think B will return?'

'I don't know, Suniti. I wish I didn't miss her quite so much.'

'Perhaps we'll dream about her.' But we don't.

*　　*　　*

We have a nightmare instead. Bit by bit the world is stripped away, the blue carpet, the walls. It peels off like so much paint. At last there is nothing left, except a small and transparent something. It is shapeless and composed of terror. It cannot penetrate the blackness round it. It cannot make any sound. But it's shrieking with the intensity of its own terror.

Luckily I wake up. I don't know who I am. After a while I see S2 beside me sitting up in bed. Then I remember. I'm supposed to be Suniti, that particular person with those preoccupations. Well, that's all right then. We fall asleep without further trouble.

*   *   *

In spite of the nightmare S2 and I are cheerful the next morning. We skip breakfast, but make ourselves a large pot of tea, and get to work at the kitchen table. We're well supplied with a number of pens and quantities of paper. It's obvious we've arrived at the same conclusion.

I write down neatly: 'Conjuring Cow'. S2 watches and nods approval.

'Now you have to address her,' S2 says. 'It's usually done.'

'Using the vocative,' I mutter to myself. 'Okay, this is what we've got: "O Cow, Baddy, Bhadravati and Bud".'

'It's not enough,' says S2, 'you have to put in all her names.'

'But I don't know all of them.'

'Well, some of them anyway. Here.'

S2 starts writing. I read it aloud: 'O Cow of a thousand faces and a thousand names, O Julia, Peter, Madeleine and Kate, O Margaret, Charlotte, Amy and S1, O

Boudicca, Sybilla, Cowslip and S2, O Ariadne, Lou-Ann and Madame X, O Cow who manifests herself in a thousand shapes and a thousand wishes . . .'

'Well?'

'Why "a thousand"?'

'It's traditional.'

'It's a bit long.'

'We have to be thorough.'

'All right, but that's just the beginning, the calling upon Cow. We haven't even got to the subject yet.'

'The subject is Cow, obviously.'

'What about us?'

'No, concentrate on her.'

'All right. So now we put in the flowery epithets?'

'Yes.'

'Like "O Celestial Surabhi, Gentle Source of Food and Fragrance"? That sort of thing?'

'No, not that sort of thing. Just what we know about her. Her attributes and qualities, what she has done and said.'

'All right. How's this? "O you who have appeared in my dreams at times with a garland of flowers about your neck, you who have sported in the woods with me, and laughed and mocked and been my friend, O you who have slain a thousand Jovians . . ." And so on. Will it do?'

'Well, it's a bit personal.'

'Prayers are personal, you know.'

'All right, but it's a bit poetic also.'

'Well, you said "flowery epithets".'

'No, you said it. The thing is, Suniti, you haven't put in her darker aspects.'

'All right. "O you who have slain a thousand Jovians, kicked up the dirt and trampled the planet; O you who have reduced me to almost nothing, then made me a present of the world and myself; O you who contain a terrible hunger, ever assuaged and feeding itself —" ' I break off. 'S2, are we suggesting that Cow is Spindle-shanks also?'

'Why not?'

'She mightn't like it.'

'Oh, Cow has a strong stomach. She won't mind.'

'But it savours of dualism or Manichaeanism . . .'

'Oh, for pity's sake, Suniti. This is no time for theological disputation. Get on with the job.'

'All right. Then have we put in enough epithets, can we make our request?'

'No, just one or two epithets more. Make them flattering this time.'

'All right. "O Cow whose tender muzzle feeds on snow peas, whose curving horns toss the sun; O Cow of the delicate bones and gentle eyes, grant us our prayer. Please return".'

'One long sentence, and one short one – I think it will

do. Come on.'

We both sit on the floor in the semi-lotus position — we can't quite manage the full lotus — and meditate hard. Our wills and minds merge.

After a while there's a clattering of hoofs like the sound of thunder. I jump up to answer the door. I fling it open. It's Cow, standing there grinning at me. I throw my arms about her neck.

I feel so very, so extraordinarily happy, I can't concentrate at all. But Cow lets herself in and makes a pot of tea. I help her. We take it into the garden.

I watch the way the light glides along her flanks, the way the short thick hairs grow on her forehead. I admire her knees, her legs, her enormous rib-cage and the shape of her head. Finally I stare at her dusty hoofs.

'Cow,' I tell her solemnly, 'I think you're a goddess.'

Cow seems amused. 'So are you, Suniti.'

I'm appalled. 'Oh no,' I exclaim. 'I make no such claims. I, really, you know, I don't have the energy.'

'But you can't help it, Suniti. You're alive, you know.'

I can see that determined look in her eye. I don't want to argue. I capitulate. 'Oh, all right, but only a minor and obscure one.'

But B hasn't been listening. She's thinking of something entirely different.

'What?' she asks. 'What were you talking about?'

'About the weather. How pleasant it is. How good it is

to have you here.'

And then Cow startles me. She says, 'I like you, Suniti.' My eyes widen.

'I like you,' I tell her with complete conviction.

'What? Even when I'm B or Baddy or Bud?'

'Even then,' I reply. But I look at Cow and add quickly, 'Even then I find you wholly engaging.' We smile at each other. But then it occurs to me that she might vanish.

'This isn't just a visit?' I ask anxiously 'You won't go away?'

I think she's going to tease, but she speaks quite kindly. 'There have been times, Suniti, when you've regarded my presence as a visitation.'

'Well, but you can be quite awful.'

But B just grins. ' "The Cow of a thousand faces and a thousand manifestations who walks rough-shod over fields and forests, and falls asleep when her day is done . . ." I'm misquoting, aren't I?' she adds penitently.

I smile at her. 'You know, I'm going to write down all this.'

'What? "The Conversations of Cow" faithfully recorded by her scribe Suniti?' B is laughing at me. I don't really mind. I go inside and get to work. On the lawn Cow grazes in the summer sun.